PETER TOPSIDE

LAST MEAL

A Deliciously Paranormal Horror Story

Last Meal

Copyright © 2024 Peter Topside

Published by Meadowsville Quill, LLC

Paperback ISBN: 979-8-9886116-3-9
Hardcover ISBN: 979-8-9886116-4-6
eISBN: 979-8-9886116-5-3

Cover and Interior Design: GKS Creative
Project Management: The Cadence Group

This is a work of fiction that contains graphic violence, strong language, and psychologically distressing elements.

All Rights Reserved. No part of this book may be reproduced or transmitted in any form or by any means, electronic or mechanical, including photocopying, recording, or by any information retrieval or storage system, without the prior written consent of the publisher.

I dedicate this book to my good buddy, Joe. You were gone too soon. I'm going to miss our weekly chats, and I'm sorry we never got the chance to have that cup of coffee. See you on the other side, my friend.

Author's Note

WHETHER YOU LOVE MY BOOKS or detest them, you have to admit they're always unique. Being a foodie really drove me to this concept, and the story just organically developed. Chuck is such a hateful character. And this was the first time I wrote solely from a first-person point of view, just letting a character spew impulsive, racist, ugly, and ignorant commentary. So it was a bit of a departure from my usual narrator-style writing, but it's always fun to try new things and really challenge myself as an author. It made me very uncomfortable to devise the content, and hopefully it will unnerve you all in just the right ways too. I also cannot emphasize enough that none of Chuck's thoughts, actions, and beliefs reflect any part of myself. Except for tasting oneself, because I'd like to think I am quite the dish. Please be aware of the use of racial slurs and homophobic slang, in addition to scenes of self-harm and cannibalism.

There are mentions throughout of a biblical event in a fictional town named Meadowsville, which is the setting of a previous trilogy I wrote. *Last Meal* takes place in the same world but does not have any other connections to the aforementioned books. It is its own unique story that can be enjoyed by itself with no prior knowledge of my other books.

Chapter 1

I loved that smell. Nothing like the odor of fresh lobster. Some regions of Maine used celery and scallions, but that just skunked the flavor. A cup of claw and knuckle meat with a little dollop of mayonnaise on top of a toasted, buttery roll, and you were in flavor country. None of that other bullshit to crowd the natural flavors. I just hoped this asshole appreciated all the effort I put into this meal.

The warden wouldn't ever let me spend over forty dollars for a last meal. Not sure if that was a national standard or just here at Eagle Stone in the esteemed Twig Valley. Some of these requests exceeded that budget, and there was nothing like telling a man on death row that his last request was denied. And I was usually the one to break the news, trying to help them figure out something more practical.

I waited at the kitchen door for the guards to escort me to Anthony DeMarco's cell.

DeMarco. Another Italian. Probably shot someone for saying *sauce* instead of *gravy*.

It's fuckin' tomato sauce, for Christ's sake. They're as bad as the niggers sometimes.

My work boots pinched my toes a bit, and my feet were achy. Long days in that kitchen, especially when I had to make last meals. And with the rate that these minorities kept rolling in, I'd always have a job.

"'Sup, Chuck. Get it? Like upchuck?" Corrections Officer Schaeffer called to me as he opened the big metal door.

Yeah, that joke never gets old. The skinniness of his neck made me want to actually puke.

"Yep. I got it. All good by me, Officer Schaeffer," I responded.

Each inhalation allowed me to see his Adam's apple protrude like there was a little creature inside, ready to burst out.

These idiots only responded if you attached their title or rank before their names. I guess it made them feel better about themselves. I think they would all die before sixty years old. They'd just keep the production line going and get another one to take their place.

"Looks like I'm taking you to see DeMarco, right?"

"Yep, I spent the last hour preparing this for him." I patted the serving tray.

"What is it?" Schaeffer took the cover off and put his face within inches of the lobster rolls.

"Why three? And where's all the celery?"

I fucking hate your face. Just let me get this to the prisoner.

"This is just a different style of making them. Little less complicated and fresh."

"Well, I'd still eat the shit out of it." He took a small piece of knuckle meat and ate it.

All that work I put into lining up the meat into equal piles on each hotdog bun was now tarnished. A bead of sweat crept down my hairline. My heart beat fast, and I gripped the tray hard enough to deform it.

"Enough," I snapped, slamming the cover onto the tray.

Schaeffer startled as he licked his fingers clean. "Okay, easy, Chucky. I'm just playing around. Let's get you to the cell," he said, eyeing me carefully.

"Thank you." I collected myself, still feeling enraged.

And only one person ever called me Chucky. And he was no longer alive. Nor should he be.

This motherfucker. Skinny piece of shit suddenly decided he wanted to eat. And he fucked up my last meal? He deserved to have his balls handcuffed to his asshole.

We walked past the prisoners toward the death row cells. The inmates hooted and hollered, smelling the meal.

"Another one bites the dust, huh, Chuck?" someone yelled.

"I'll suck your cock if you give me a meal like that. Might do it even if you don't."

They all knew me. I made and served all the food that went out to all five hundred inmates. That chubby guy with the receding hairline in the kitchen serving all the shit they thought was behind them from high school cafeterias. The usual slop like powdered eggs, frozen pizza, fish patties, and other highly processed food. No creativity. No heart. Just making tons of food to feed these hungry prisoners.

But these guys couldn't be picky. They were getting three nutritionally sound meals each day. Guaranteed. If it were up to me, they'd all be fucking dead. It would be nothing but death row inmates here. I wouldn't have to wait weeks to months between last meals. That was where I shined. I was the last freedom they got before death. Just being a part of the process was special to me. Most people looked down on me for having this job, but I took great pride in it. The attention always went to the wardens, guards, and inmates. No one ever heard about the prison cooks.

And some of these lower-level correctional facilities used inmates to cook. Cooking was a privilege. These scumbags didn't deserve to be in the kitchen like me. They all made their choices, and that was why they were incarcerated. *Rot in a cell.*

The prison was decked out in mostly grays. Gray bars, gray walls, and gray floors. Nothing but gray. Not just for appearances, but also a state of mind too.

Schaeffer stopped and put his hand out, almost making me drop the platter. "Whoa ho there, Big Chuck." He patted my abdomen.

I hope you get eaten by one of these animals. There's gotta be a cannibal or two in here.

A smaller man sat on the tiny bed in his cell. His head was in his hands, with his longer hair hanging down over his face.

"Chuck Saunders. I believe you know of Mr. Anthony DeMarco. Convicted of first-degree manslaughter. Five victims. Sentenced to death tomorrow morning by lethal injection."

DeMarco looked up at us. He wasn't crying, but it looked to start any minute. "I didn't mean to do it. They said they'd hurt my family if I didn't," he pleaded.

Sure, you didn't. Only sorry because you got caught, you greasy wop.

Schaeffer showed no empathy or compassion. "Prisoner, stand against the far wall, facing away from us."

DeMarco slowly stood up and walked between the metal toilet and sink, turning his back. The chains securing him to the floor rattled. Schaeffer entered ahead of me and removed his baton in case the prisoner decided to make a move. Luckily, he stayed still.

"Mr. DeMarco, I present your last meal," I said, placing it on a small wooden tray, removing the top. The smell of the lobster permeated the entire cell, and DeMarco took note of the aroma.

"Prisoner, please sit and start your meal," Schaeffer called out.

DeMarco turned around and took his seat. He looked up at me, almost looking to me for counsel, but Schaeffer and I just observed.

"Are you just going to stand there and watch me?" he asked indignantly.

"You have silverware and a metal tray, inmate. What do you think?" Schaeffer responded.

Just eat the food and tell me it's good.

DeMarco picked up the lobster roll and took a big bite. The mayo smeared around his mouth, and a little bit of butter dripped onto the tray. The man sighed and looked to be content in the moment.

That's it. Enjoy your last meal. The last bit of delight that you'll ever have. And it's all thanks to me.

"How is it?" I asked.

"I'm eating it, aren't I?" he snapped back.

You disrespectful little fuck. I hope you feel every bit of that poison enter your body. I hope it hurts, and I hope you think of me right before everything goes black. I fucking hate you.

"Saunders." Schaeffer patted me forcibly on the back. "You okay?"

Yeah, between you and DeMarco, I feel like I'm the luckiest guy in the world. Note the sarcasm, skinny.

"I'm fine."

"Do you want me to have someone escort you back?"

"No, I want to watch."

DeMarco made quick work of the three lobster rolls and then ate the packaged chocolate chip cookie in a few bites. He sat back in the chair, obviously full, but showed no emotion. All that was left was the last rites before he was put to death tomorrow.

Schaeffer ordered the prisoner back against the far wall, and he collected all the silverware and the tray, handing them off to me.

They never say thank you. I've done this hundreds of times over the years and it's a rarity. You're welcome, you smug little cocksucker. Enjoy your death tomorrow. You deserve every bit of it.

"Thank you," I heard before exiting the cell.

I turned around and saw DeMarco still against the wall. I didn't respond but was shaken at his words. Maybe I was wrong about him?

Chapter 2

My tiny studio apartment looked untouched. Spotless, organized, and cozy. Exactly how it should be.

My cat, Renegade, slept on the arm of my two-seated couch. I bought this little bastard a cat house and a bed to sleep on, and he chose this instead. He was a patchwork of whites, browns, and blacks. Charred and burned. Looked like someone cooked a piece of chicken wrong.

I took off my shoes and slammed them on the ground. Renegade didn't budge. He only moved when I gave him food. His expensive, limited-ingredient food. I took the can off the counter and opened the top. The cat opened an eye and lifted an ear. As soon as the minced tuna flopped into the bowl, the animal was gone. He stood at my leg and howled like he hadn't eaten in weeks.

"I fed you before I left this morning, you little asshole." I brought it to his feeding tray.

The cat put its face into the food and gorged without any appreciation. He never said thank you to me either. He was no better than those shitbags at the prison. They all just snorted and grunted, taking no time to think about the person who prepared and served them their food.

I picked up the can to wash it out before tossing into the recycling bin, and a sharp pain radiated through my finger. The thin metal protuberance of the lid cut my pointer finger deep. The blood dripped down my hand and onto the counter.

"Shit," I said, grabbing a paper towel and a small bowl. "I can't waste this."

I grabbed the finger and squeezed hard, getting as much blood out as possible before the wound clotted. The bowl filled with about a tablespoon of blood before it stopped.

"Better than nothing." I washed my hands and dried them with a paper towel.

I opened the fridge and found the defrosted ribeye, just waiting for me to toss into the skillet. No matter how many dishes I made or how many times I turned on the stovetop, it excited me to no end. Food was my life.

I prepared two small skillets, one with the steak and the other for the mushroom sauce.

The steak was tossed onto high heat with some salt and pepper on both sides. I then minced some garlic and sliced mushrooms, tossing them into some vegetable oil over medium-high heat. It sizzled and filled the room with a delicious aroma. Next the butter, some tarragon, then the beef stock and white wine. I'd made this mushroom sauce so many times that it was like second nature to me nowadays.

I used my trusty plastic spatula, tossing everything together, waiting for the sauce to reduce. I flipped the steak once and salivated at the crust on the meat. But would I be able to finish both at same time? I couldn't eat a cold fucking steak with a hot sauce. It'd taste like shit. And the steak would continue cooking, so it'd be more medium-well than medium.

"Come on, you fuck," I reprimanded the food.

I took the blood and poured it into the sauce. The sauce thickened slightly as the blood mixed in undetected.

Renegade watched me with his dead eyes. Those undeserving eyes.

"This isn't for you. You've had your food. And this is mine," I said.

But he continued watching for another few seconds, before grooming his paws.

I plated the steak and poured over the blood mushroom sauce. Dinner was served. I cut into the steak and took a bite. It was creamy, perfectly seasoned, with just a little bite from the blood. Not the normal uncooked irony flavor, but a more subtle undertone of something a little sweet. But the balance was perfect. Another culinary accomplishment. Not the first time I've cooked with blood, my own included, but this was one of the better inclusions to date. I had to keep learning and keep trying new things. There were culinary masters all over the world. I'd never be to that level. It was so oversaturated with talent that I'd have a better chance of being struck by lightning a dozen times. No, I was carving out a new niche. And if it took me using my own body to achieve greatness in an entirely new way, then I was more than willing to do so.

Anyway, it was all good sport. I needed to be at my best to assist those death row inmates in their final wish before they transitioned. Like an angel of death. They were happy to see me but knew that it was the last pleasant experience of their life.

Renegade rolled onto his side and stared at the wall as I finished eating my dinner.

Chapter 3

I hated working with all these uppity spics. They shouldn't be allowed in my kitchen. It was a privilege to be in here with me. Their hairnets were on wrong, and they weren't even washing their hands. One of them had a cigarette hanging out of his mouth.

"You filthy fucks," I muttered, as I flipped the giant pile of artificial eggs onto the large griddle.

One of the younger Hispanic inmates, Ramirez, tossed the dishes down in the sink. "You say something, hombre?"

I turned around and picked up the one butcher knife. "Maybe I did. You wanna make something of it, short stack?" I was tired of these assholes. Couldn't even wash dishes without talking shit. Especially the Latinos. They were all so loud and wouldn't shut up.

"*Si, lo que sea, loco tonto blanco,*" Ramirez said under his breath to me. Yeah, whatever, you crazy white fool. "*Maldito punk blanco.*" Damn white punk.

That's right. Keep running your mouth. One day maybe you'll do something dumb to the wrong person, and I'll be serving you some rat shit tacos before they hang you like a flag.

"You are crazy, you know that?" inmate Conti called out as he slopped down huge servings of oatmeal onto each tray. "You ain't even a prisoner. Why are you here?"

"Let's just say it's my passion," I replied, putting the cooked scrambled eggs into a large steam tray and carrying it over to Conti's serving station.

The line of prisoners looked endless. Some days I tried to see if I could detect a pattern. Right now, I saw a black, a mocha, and two whites. Nope, still no discernable pattern.

"I don't like eggs," the one inmate called out.

"Then starve, you white trash," I said loud enough to hear. All these complaints and no one appreciated a free fucking meal.

"Calm down," Conti said. "No use crying over some powdered eggs, Chuck."

I didn't respond. There was no need to. I didn't need to have playful banter with any of these crumbums.

"When's DeMarco getting put down?" I asked, eager to watch the process. The time was 10:40 a.m.

"I think eleven. Why?" Washington asked.

"I feel it's my responsibility to be there when it happens."

"That's a little strange."

I ignored him.

"Not trying to pick on ya, but you're just a prison cook."

I grabbed Washington by the scruff and pushed him into the one oven, knocking over some pans. They clanged upon landing on the floor.

"Okay, okay, I'm sorry," he said, putting his hands up.

Two guards entered the kitchen, and they pulled me away. I brushed their hands off of me. I shouldn't be manhandled like a prisoner. Because I wasn't one. And never would be. I then noticed the end of the chow line was in sight.

"Ramirez, Conti, Washington, and the rest of you pond scum. Scrape the griddle, mop the floors, take the trash out, and make my kitchen look like new before lunch," I barked.

I didn't hear any of them respond. Who cared. God forbid they did some hard work and not get accolades. The whole world would crumble. Pussies.

I tossed my apron onto the counter. It had a rainbow of stains on it, with sweat, blood, grease, and ash making it a beautiful representation of the work I put in each day. *All for this unappreciative gutter trash. I'm glad this is the last prison in the United States to allow outlawed execution methods. Good to know justice can still be served.*

A hand landed on my shoulder. From the bony structure and the specific grip, I knew it belonged to Schaeffer. I became a little rattled at how accustomed I was to his touch. Not too hard but also not uncomfortable. I was no fag either. What a dumb thought. I wouldn't touch a dick if it was with someone else's hand.

I'm as straight as an uncooked piece of spaghetti. And I taste better too.

"You want me to escort you to the execution chamber?" he asked in a sly voice.

"Yes."

"What's the magic word?"

"Please." I resisted the urge to punch him.

But what chance would I stand? I got away with it against the prisoners only because the warden had a low tolerance for misbehaving. And he was always ready to punish his inmates. So they cowered to me, and the guards would break it up before anyone did anything serious. I needed to show dominance in my domain to keep the upper hand around here. In that kitchen, I was God, as far as they were all concerned.

Schaeffer escorted me through the penitentiary—quiet, as everyone was in the meal hall. We entered the viewing room, and one of the newer officers was strapping DeMarco onto a gurney. A physician was carefully inserting cannulas into each arm. An EKG monitor was also set up, with the electrode pads being placed across DeMarco's hairy chest.

The saline solution began to drip, and the inmate shook uncontrollably. "I didn't want to do it. You have to believe me."

No one reacted. Not the officers in the room, anyone in the small audience in the viewing room, the physician. Not anyone.

An officer loaded the three syringes and secured them into the IVs.

Warden Monroe walked in, sporting a dark blue business suit. Always dressed to the nines. Probably to distract from his embarrassing lisp.

The room settled and the procedure was about to begin.

"Anthony DeMarco. Found guilty of first-degree manslaughter to be put to death by lethal injection. Do you have any final statement to make?"

DeMarco looked at the audience and found me. There was no question he was focused on me and nothing else. This had never happened before. Usually, they watched their wives or family members of those who were affected by their terrible actions. No one ever watched me. I was unseen.

"I'm sorry for everything. I know I was wrong. And if I could take it all back, I would."

Sure, sure. Suddenly they found forgiveness in hope of God taking mercy on them.

The warden nodded at the officer, who proceeded to manually inject each of the three drugs in a sequence. The barbiturate knocked them out, the muscle relaxer caused the paralysis of their respiratory muscles, and finally, the potassium chloride triggered an abnormal and fatal heartbeat.

DeMarco kept his eyes on me. His body tensed briefly but then relaxed. The EKG rhythm sped up but then began to prolong with each beat. As I saw his eyes start to close, his tongue glanced over his lower lip, as if he were hungry. What was that?

Several minutes went by, and his body went limp. The EKG was flat. Anthony DeMarco was dead.

I wanted to feel sad, but I didn't. He was a killer. Nothing else mattered. A sin resolved. He would never hurt anyone else again. But why was he so intent on staring me down?

I stood up, ready to go prep for lunch. Hopefully, those idiots in the kitchen were almost done scrubbing it all down. Still an ugly, shitty kitchen, but at least it'd be clean.

Suddenly, the entire compound shook. A bright light entered every window in the prison. It lasted for a few seconds, disorienting everyone. Then it was gone as quickly as it started.

What the fuck was that?

Out of the corner of my eye, I saw DeMarco stand up and run off. I looked to the gurney, but his body was still there.

How was that possible? What had just happened?

Chapter 4

Today's last meal was for a prisoner named Bob Higgins. What a shitty name. Imagine someone called him Bobby Higgins growing up. Sounded like a pedophile's dream. "Bobby Higgins, come into my creepy basement to see my supposed train collection."

The possibilities were endless. Poor guy. I almost felt bad for him. Almost. A shitty end to a shitty life. At least he'd get a special meal in before the end.

Officer Schaeffer walked in with a meal request paper. "Here ya go, Chuck. Not your usual request," he said passing it to me.

But there was nothing on it.

"What is this, a joke?"

"No joke. He doesn't wanna eat again. He claims he just wants to die."

I crumpled up the paper and threw it toward the open garbage, missing it by a few inches.

"At least you're a damn fine cook," Schaeffer added in, testing my patience. "But don't ever try to play basketball. And, if you do, don't be on my team."

"I don't understand. They always want a final meal," I said, in a bit of a panic now.

Schaeffer put his hands up, attempting to deescalate me.

I started to pace around the kitchen a bit. "Can I speak with him?"

"You want to talk to him? About what?"

"He should understand the importance of a last meal, that's why. It's the last positive thing he'll experience before death. He should want it. I'll prepare whatever he wants!"

Schaffer took a step back and watched me. "I . . . uh . . . guess . . . but make it quick." He motioned for me to follow.

I grabbed a gingersnap from the pile that I baked fresh the previous day for the dinner line tonight. This idiot should at least taste something I made so he'd know how good it was.

"So that was some shit yesterday with that lightning bolt out of Meadowsville, right? Shook the hell outta me and just about everyone else. They're saying it was a biblical event of some kind. But that town is so fucked up. Who knows. Maybe it was aliens or something. Haven't talked to anyone who didn't see that light."

I wasn't overly concerned about Meadowsville. It'd been the laughingstock of the country for decades. Monsters, ghouls, and whatever other bullshit they made up to keep the tourism numbers up. Couldn't believe a single word of it.

Schaeffer brought me to the containment area and opened the cell, letting us both in. Higgins was a heavyset gentleman with Droopy Dog eyes and a long face.

"What the hell is this?" he barked out, standing up.

"Prisoner, stand down and take your seat. This is the prison chef who wants to speak with you about your unwillingness to accept a last meal," Schaeffer commanded.

Higgins stood for a few seconds, sporting an uncertain look, before sitting slowly. "I don't understand. I said I don't wanna eat. I'll be dead tomorrow anyway. What's the problem?"

I stepped forward. "Because this is bigger than you. It allows everyone at the prison and outside of these walls to acknowledge your death and soften the blow for all those affected by it. And it also brings you some degree of comfort. It is also sort of a small celebration of your life, too. And it gives you one final special request. The last one you'll ever have. A reminder of what you enjoyed in your life. Friends, family, whatever else. Food is a powerful thing."

"I don't want it," he said smugly. "I'm not hungry. Who would be before being executed?"

I started to sweat a bit and get angry. "How about this. Try this cookie and tell me if you like it or not. From there, we can talk further. I think you'll reconsider." I picked up the small plate.

"I said I don't wanna eat anything. Are you deaf?"

I tightened my grip on the plate, unsure if it would crack or not. I couldn't believe he would refuse a delicious treat like this. A nice offering and gesture, and he just wouldn't have it.

"I think you should reconsider."

"I think you should shove it up your ass."

My control started to waver. "How about this. Take one bite, and if it's not the tastiest cookie you've ever had, I'll leave the room and you can be left alone. However, I don't think that'll be the case."

Schaeffer modified his stance, putting a hand on his baton. "Chuck, it's enough. I don't think he wants it."

"Try it," I implored, pushing the plate across the table to him.

Higgins looked at the plate and pushed it to the floor, shattering it. The cookie remained intact.

You obnoxious piece of shit. You're gonna regret that.

I slowly picked up the cookie, grabbed him by the hair, and shoved it into his mouth. "How's that taste? Pretty goddamned good now, isn't it?" I felt his spit on my fingers, and he struggled to get up, but I held him in place.

"Jesus Christ, Chuck, that's enough," Schaeffer said from behind me, trying to pull me off.

I didn't let my grip falter. Higgins, despite his size, was completely overpowered. I wasn't even breaking a sweat. I liked the intensity. These scummy prisoners should be thankful I was here. I was above them in every single way. Fucking scumbag garbage like this would not disrespect me.

"Chuck, I'm gonna pop you in the fuckin' head if you don't let him go," Schaeffer muttered through clenched teeth.

I got it. I'd overstepped once again. But this facility gave its officers and staff a lot of leeway. Schaeffer wouldn't report this, and Higgins was on death row. It wouldn't go anywhere.

I let go, and Higgins spit the cookie out. "You'll fuckin' hang for this, you faggot." He stood up.

Schaeffer let me go and slammed Higgins back down into the metal chair.

"Not before you. Enjoy your last night, prisoner." Schaeffer pulled me out of the room, slamming and locking the cell door.

He pinned me against the wall and got nose-to-nose with me. "What do you think you're doing? You can't touch the prisoners."

I realized none of these inmates were worth me jeopardizing my job, so I yielded to him. "Sorry, he just got me all fucked up. I apologize for my outburst." I didn't mean a word of it.

Schaeffer backed up from me and gave me an uncertain look. He didn't appreciate my insincerity.

"Shall we just assume that the Meadowsville incident has you a little uneasy?" he asked, trying to find some sort of logic to scrub the incident.

"Yeah, let's go with that," I responded, not caring what happened in that shitty town. I was just sorry that the whole fucking place didn't get scorched.

"Let's get you back to the kitchen before lunchtime hits." He guided me back.

I didn't care. I'd be there front and center when Higgins hanged tomorrow.

Chapter 5

I watched the inmates pulling out the huge sleeves of white bread. And the bologna. And the apples. And little bags of chips. And a small bottle of vegetable juice. An ugly little meal, but that was what my instructions were. I think the Federal Bureau of Prisons set the standards. That was why last meals were also called special meals. They fed these inmates dog-shit food. But if they were lucky enough to be on death row, they could pick anything they wanted, as long as it was under forty dollars. And that allowed me to get really creative. Use all of the tools I'd learned. Self-taught. Because, when I was a kid, I wasn't allowed to use the kitchen. Couldn't even open the freezer until I was eighteen years old. But I couldn't complain. Plenty of other people had it worse than me growing up.

My prick father had some weird idiosyncrasies about the kitchen. Never cared to ask about them. Didn't think he would've been honest about it either. He forced my mother, that poor woman, to cook like a slave. Never thanked her or showed any appreciation. He'd even yell at me for trying to bring my dishes to the sink.

"That's her job, Chucky," he'd say to me. Like he was trying to give me some sage advice.

Then she died and I left home. Worked in horrible little nothing jobs for years, scrubbing restaurants, watching the various chefs cook, and learning the trade.

Some chefs were better than others. Especially their attitudes. You could always tell the ones who just got their bachelor's in culinary arts or some other random certification. They had chips on their shoulders. Like, because they held those little pieces of paper, they were better than everyone else. And their cooking was never bad, but also not all that creative either. It was always the unaccredited cooks who fascinated me. The ones who cooked with busted equipment, lower-quality food, inadequate help, but somehow still found a way to make it all work. They created magic in those kitchens. And no one ever even knew they existed. Just a faceless person in the shielded kitchen. The waitstaff, cashiers, managers, and all the other staff got the credit. But never the chef. The only time he heard anything was if a customer wanted to send something back. Disrespectful.

So I worked my way up, from scrubbing floors after hours to prepping to assisting to doing the actual cooking, and finally I felt confident enough to be the lead chef. But I had no credentials, so I was limited. Just a hardworking kid with the dream of doing something special. After two decades honing my skills and working in almost two dozen restaurants, I was lucky enough to land the job in Eagle Stone Correctional Facility. Steady work, good pay, great benefits, and it allowed me to be creative with the last meals. That was my favorite part. But the food took hold of my life. It was everything to me. I wanted to be the best and, goddamn it, I would be the best. I would make myself into something special one day.

My attention came back from my memories to the kitchen aides.

"How many sandwiches we got?"

"Two hundred?"

"Two hundred!"

"Couldn't have been one hundred eighty-seven?"

"Why one hundred eighty-seven?"

"So I could clap yo' ass out and be done with all this fuckin' mystery meat."

I chuckled. My crew had their moments. But they were all here just to take orders from me. Below me in the pecking order. And I was left alone to prepare final meals. No one was allowed in here when I worked. I needed to focus and not be bothered. Schaeffer somehow was always here. Guy lived for overtime, and he kept a close eye on me. Not sure why.

I noticed that Anthony DeMarco was staring at me from across the kitchen. How was he here? *He's dead.* That smirk. His skin a sickly green. The veins all over his body protruding. And his face sunken in like a Tim Burton creation.

This can't be real. He can't be here. But there he was. And how did no one else notice him? He licked his lips again. His tongue looked like a dead snake. Then he winked. I looked down. It couldn't be real. Maybe the incident with Higgins just shook me up a little. I didn't sleep well again last night. I saw DeMarco die. He couldn't be here.

I looked up again, and he was still there watching me intently.

"You can't be here!" I yelled impulsively.

Ramirez, Conti, and Washington all stopped and looked at me.

"You all right, Chuck?" Conti asked.

"He just being a racist fuck again," Ramirez called out. "Chuck, you touch me again, I'll toss you on the stovetop and scorch ya like they about to do to Higgins." He took two knives and tried to perform a few karate moves but dropped both. He shrugged it off. "Fuck these knives. Got all the power I need here." He brandished his fists.

"Sure, sure, Ramirez. You little Latino bug," Washington tossed out.

I shook my head, distracted by my three aides, and then noticed DeMarco was gone.

"Chuck, am I stacking the bologna the right way or you gonna freak again?" Conti asked.

I looked at his perfectly aligned sandwiches. "Yeah, all good, Conti. Good work." I tried to collect myself.

"See, you just gotta be white like me for Chuck to be nice to ya. Hear that, boys?"

Washington and Ramirez laughed.

But how could DeMarco be here? *What the fuck is going on with me?*

Chapter 6

I stood at the window with several others. We all looked outside at the executioner as the burly man fitted the rope around Higgins's neck. Higgins shifted his head and just stood there with his eyes closed. His arms and legs were strapped together. Warden Monroe used a small microphone to announce the sentence to the audience. The three men stood in the designated hanging area atop a well-preserved wooden platform. The entire ceiling allowed the sun in. Such brightness for such a dark occasion.

I couldn't wait to see Higgins's body swaying in the wind. Obnoxious fuck. Not making him a last meal really irritated me. We had a steady stream of prisoners come in for death row, mainly because this facility used outlawed executive methods. And we got everyone else's problems. But it was rare when someone said no to a last meal. I would've been less insulted if they asked for a meal from an outside source. How did someone on death row not see how special that final meal was?

Higgins started crying. "Please no . . . God no . . . I don't deserve this. Someone help me."

I heard the warden speaking, but I was lost in my thoughts. Who cared what Higgins was convicted of. It was more than enough to sentence him to death, so that was all that mattered.

The warden waved his hand, the big wooden lever was pulled, and Higgins's ample frame dropped through opening in the platform. His face turned apple red.

Apples were so good. Either on their own, as a side dish, part of a main course, breakfast, or dessert. Very versatile. And there were so many of them.

Higgins swung as his body convulsed briefly, then it stopped. I was surprised his neck didn't break before he suffocated. And he died crying like a little baby. No one in the room around me reacted.

Warden Monroe stood there, resembling a ghoul. No judgment, no pity, no sense of anything. His thin, bony frame pushed against his suit.

The tears dripped down Higgin's face, plopping onto the sand underneath the wooden platform. They didn't stop though. It was as if he were still alive. Everyone began to leave the room, but I stayed put. Higgins was cut down, and the rope was pulled off his elongated neck. The skin was stretched, bruised, and burned from the rope. They began loading the body onto a gurney to transport to the crematorium. I stood there watching in anticipation of something like DeMarco happening again. I turned to leave and saw Higgins standing by the door.

His eyes were bloodshot, his face still as red as a stop sign, and his neck looked like a horror show. He smiled at me.

What the fuck is this?

I ran out of the room.

Chapter 7

That night, I stood over my stove. The thoughts of DeMarco and Higgins flooded through my mind. Their... well... spirits, spooks, ghosts, or whatever the hell they're called. *Apparitions* sounded classy, right? Well, anyway, they were stalking me. But why?

The venison burger in the cast iron skillet spattered a bit. Renegade looked up at the sound. That little furball would just lick the grease up anyway. Why bother cleaning anymore? He ate dust, grease, crumbs, and anything else.

I flipped the burger, a beautiful deep brown crust on the bottom. A perfect cook. Four more minutes and it'd be showtime. The mushrooms were already sauteed and the butter knife had a generous dollop of creamy brie on it. I loved the anticipation of the assembly.

As the burger finished frying, I used my weathered rubber spatula and placed it carefully on the slightly toasted wheat bun. I smothered the top with brie, then the mushrooms, and hit it with a little kiss of mayo. I placed the top portion of the bun on and took a minute to admire it.

"Gorgeous," I said to myself, feeling a bit emotional. "Absolutely gorgeous."

I thought back to the kitchen at my parents' house. My mother was allowed to cook only select items. Never anything different. No venison, no fish, not even meatloaf. Dad wouldn't allow that to happen. Part of me should thank him for depriving me of high-quality foods all those years. Made me want it more. Made me hungrier and more motivated to have it. Not like the kids with wealthier parents, who would have Wagyu burgers and rack of lamb and all sorts of foods that I wouldn't taste until I was several decades into my life. But no one had control over me now.

I turned back to the stove to wipe up some of the grease. I suddenly saw Higgins's beet-red face within inches of me. His eyes burned through me, and I was frozen in place. It scared me to the core.

Renegade hissed and hid under the couch.

I stumbled back, tripping into the counter, but the ghost was already gone. Not caring that my hand was gripping the hot skillet, I double checked that the burger was unharmed. Thank the good lord it wasn't.

LAST MEAL

I removed my hand off the skillet, leaving a few little pieces of skin on it. I've burned and cut my hands so many times over the years that I don't have much feeling in them anymore. Instinctively I put my palm against my lips, tasting the charred flesh. Maybe it was from the venison grease, but my hand tasted really great. Not just good, but great. To avoid an infection, I quickly washed my hands.

Why was Higgins here? Renegade saw it too. It wasn't just in my imagination. These spirits were actually following me.

Maybe I'm not crazy?

Chapter 8

I went in to work early this morning. Started my twelve-hour day ahead of schedule. Nothing to do at home besides watch Renegade piss in his litterbox every few hours.

I scanned into the facility and went down the long hallway to the kitchen. It was dark, and no one would be in there for at least another hour. I walked in and turned the lights on.

Higgins and DeMarco stood there waiting for me.

I felt unsure of the situation, but I wouldn't let a bunch of these inmates scare me, whether alive or dead. "What do you want from me?" I asked calmly.

They looked at one another.

"I saw you both die. You shouldn't be here." I stood my ground.

"Why are you so hateful and angry, Chuck?" Higgins asked.

I always knew that about myself but had never heard anyone actually say it before this moment.

"The things in your mind that come outta that filthy mouth of yours. Just not right," DeMarco joined in.

This amused me now. "So what, are you guys gonna haunt me and make me change my ways? You know that Dickens's *Christmas Carol* was made up, right? Not fuckin' real."

DeMarco looked down and shook his head.

"We're not here to change anything," Higgins added as his head moved around oddly.

"In fact, we might just be here to speed things up," his partner brought in.

"The fuck does that mean, you silly spooks? Well, at least you're both white. I have enough minorities haunting my life. Don't need their ghosts bothering me after hours too." I pushed these entities out of my mind and started preparing for breakfast service.

"Why are you here?" Higgins asked.

"I could ask you both the same thing."

"Why do you take pleasure in hurting others? And watching others in pain?" Demarco added.

I paused for a moment, unsure if I needed to respond any further. "This act is getting a little old. Why don't you guys ask God for forgiveness and float into the afterlife. Or whatever happens. I don't know. Don't care. Not my problem."

"Oh, but it is, Chucky." DeMarco threw a butcher knife at me, barely missing my head.

"The hell you do that for, Casper?" I looked at the broken blade.

"Wherever you are, wherever you go, we'll be there. Watching you. And more will come. It's up to you how far this has to go."

I didn't like the attempt to rattle me. "That sounds like that shitty song by the Police. Sting was better on his own. Nice try though. When you got nothing to lose, you can't get scared."

DeMarco grabbed my hand and slammed it down on the counter. Higgins took a large serrated knife out of the cutting block nearby and rested it on my knuckles.

"Oh, you've got plenty to lose. Lots of fingers. A nose. A tongue. All the lovely little body parts that let you cook and eat. Where would you be without them?"

Now I was angry. Food was everything to me. I hadn't been this scared since I used to hide in my closet during one of my father's rampages. And I promised myself that once I was out of there, I would never let anyone intimidate me again.

"Go ahead, you undead mick. Cut me into pieces. I dare ya. You think I'll let a couple of inmates get under my skin. Fuck you." I defiantly spat at the ghosts.

The kitchen door opened, and Schaeffer walked in slowly. "'Sup, Chuck?"

I nodded.

"You . . . uh . . . talking to someone in here?"

"Yeah, sorry, I was just thinking out loud."

"You've been acting different lately. Everything okay?"

I took a bit of offense to him prodding. "I'm fine. Last person I'd talk about my problems to is a cop."

He rolled his eyes. "Just checking on ya, you paranoid fuck. You're lucky I'm your assigned guard. Any of these other animals I work with would have left you a stain on the wall." He walked off.

Fuck him too. Unprofessional rent-a-cop.

A few minutes later, Conti, Ramirez, and Washington walked in to help me start cooking.

"Hola, Chuck."

"Hey, Chuck."

"Chuckster..."

Such warm greetings from such an amazing trio of inmates. *Note the sarcasm.*

Chapter 9

A few days passed and things went back to where they were. No ghosts, no issues, and, dare I say, a decent patch? Hopefully, I didn't jinx myself.

Schaeffer walked in and handed me a small slip of paper. Another request for a special meal. We'd done this same interaction so many times before.

"Whatta we got here?" I asked.

"Another one bites the dust. Or soon will bite the dust. Real nasty character. Aurelio Bazalar. Raped and ate a dozen women. Maybe more, but they only could prove twelve. They call him the Casanova Cannibal."

"Most spics are nasty characters," I muttered.

"You know my wife is Guatemalan, right?" Schaeffer sized me up.

I thought back to the last few years he and I had worked together. I thought they divorced at some point. I had to spin this into a lighter situation.

"She left you, didn't she? Probably could've picked any name out of the phone book and done better."

"And what's your wife's . . . oh, that's right. No woman in your life. Maybe if you had someone boppin' your salami around a few times a month, you'd lighten up a bit. Not pull knives on inmates for using the wrong cooking utensil or whatever."

Oof, that stung a little.

I could work with this. "I'm gay," I replied, hoping to silence my antagonist.

Ramirez heard me and blurted out, "Even better, you chunk of white bread. Already broken in for me."

Conti, Ramirez, and Washington all cracked up.

"Okay, I'm not gay, but boy did that shut you up quick," I said as Schaeffer walked away, clearly frustrated.

"You have one hour to make his meal. Finish up breakfast service and get to it, chef," Schaeffer left for a cigarette break.

"An hour? I can't do much of anything in an hour."

"You'll see . . ." Schaeffer shut the door.

I looked down at the list. It read *uncooked London broil*. That was it. No prep. No anything.

Washington looked over my shoulder. "Gonna be a real short prep for this guy."

I had a lot of feelings about this request. I couldn't deny this man his special meal. But he really liked raw meat? I needed to know why. The curiosity almost overshadowed the dissatisfaction that I had nothing to bake or cook for Bazalar. Just defrost a chunk of meat and toss on a plate for him.

An hour and several cold-water baths later, there was a two-pound chunk of raw London broil sitting on a plate. Schaeffer walked in, and we continued the routine, bringing the special meal to the inmate. The prison never changed, all the inmates in their cells just biding their time. The common area was messy but still fairly nice, with a few couches, and some TVs hanging high on the walls. Then there was the library, the chapel, and the administration offices.

We arrived at Aurelio's cell, which was in the death-row section. He was a solid Hispanic man in his early forties. Clean-shaven with a very tight haircut. His eyes lit up when he saw the meal in my hands. Made me feel good. Might be a bit unorthodox, but I liked a new challenge.

Schaeffer called out, "Inmate, hands on the far wall. Do not move until I tell you." We entered, placing the plate on the metal table. Schaeffer guided the prisoner back to the metal chair, ensuring his harness was bolted into the floor. But his hands were freed.

"*Dios es grande. Dios es bueno. Agradezcámosle por nuestros alimentos. Por sus manos todos somos alimentados. Te agradecemos por nuestro pan de cada día. Amén.*" God is great. God is good. Let us thank Him for our food. For by His hands we all are fed. We thank You for our daily bread.

Aurelio ripped into the meat with an amazing ferocity. This was not his first time doing this.

I immediately had a ton of questions for him.

"Schaeffer, can I have a minute with the prisoner?"

Schaeffer looked at me. "I don't think I can do that, Chuck."

"Please, I've never had this sort of request before. I just have some questions for him. Please, do me this favor. I'll stop saying *spic* in front of you, if you do," I pleaded.

He gripped his vest and entered into a deep thought. "Two minutes. No more. No less."

As he left, I was glued to this man. Ready to die but completely enamored with this raw meat. Nothing else mattered to him but this meal. It was a high compliment to me.

"Aurelio, is it?"

The man looked up at me, covered in blood and meat bits. He licked his fingers and then chewed off one of his nails.

"What's it like?"

"What?" He swallowed another clump of the meat.

A few drops of blood dripped on the floor.

"Human meat."

He stopped eating and looked at me deeply. Deep into my soul.

"Food is my everything. I've never had it. But I think I might want to." I briefly recalled all of my previous efforts using my own body as ingredients. So satisfying, for some reason.

Aurelio unleashed a devilish grin on his bloodied face. "The meat is divine. Raw is great. But a talented chef could really do something special with it, I'm sure."

That put loads of ideas in my head. I'd put my nails, blood, and pieces of skin into some of my own meals. Sometimes intentional, other times not. But always for myself. No one else should have the pleasure of devouring me. For me and only me.

"Do you enjoy killing people?"

"I don't hate it. But worth it for the meat. You haven't lived until you've had human meat."

I smiled so big that I thought my cheeks ripped.

"Aurelio, I wish you the best of luck with your transition tomorrow. And it was my pleasure to prepare this meal for you."

As I stood up, I noticed Higgins and DeMarco standing in the far corners, just observing our interaction. Maybe they were judging me for my questions. Or maybe shocked that I had a pleasant interaction with a minority for once. I didn't plan on making it a habit.

I knocked on the door, knowing Schaeffer was nearby. Aurelio ate the rest of the meat. He sat there and watched me. I had a feeling this wouldn't be the last time I saw this inmate. This savage prisoner was equally beautiful and gruesome.

Chapter 10

The next day, Aurelio was strapped into an electric chair. I felt I owed it to my prisoners to be present for each execution. The executioner put the belt across his chest, groin, legs, and arms. The metal skullcap was lowered onto his head, covering a moistened cloth. The warden was present and read off the charges and chosen method of execution. Like we all didn't see what was right in front of us.

The switch was pulled, and Aurelio watched me through the viewing window. His body shook and steamed as the currents ate through his nervous system. Like watching a live animal be cooked. A tear came down my cheek, as this elicited a great deal of emotion from me. It was such a beautiful process to be a part of. The two minutes went by too quickly. The lever was pulled back up, and Aurelio's body stopped moving.

I bet it smelled wonderful in that room. My stomach gurgled. It brought me back to all those nights that I refused to eat dinner because I didn't want to eat with my parents. Well, my mother was fine, but she was a package deal with my father.

I stood up to return to duty in the kitchen and saw Aurelio in the hallway. It was no surprise, being my third time now. Didn't seem fair that he was killed in the chair. He preferred raw meat, and he was cooked on his way out. I felt like there was a moral issue here.

The ghost's skin was well done, especially around his eyes, hairline, and hands.

I went back to the kitchen and prepped for lunch service. Mystery meatloaf, powdered mashed potatoes, frozen discount vegetables, and an orange. What a disgusting combination of shit-quality food. But my job was to just serve and not think much. Except for those special meals. But Aurelio's final meal and our chat really had my mind working overtime.

As I flipped a few slabs of meatloaf on the grill top, the pungent odor of whatever chunks of rancid roadkill it had mixed in activated my olfactory sense. I was about to gag, but I was also one to cook with my own bodily fluids, so it never got to that point. *Hypocrite much?*

I noticed someone standing over me, and I turned to see Aurelio's blistered face. I looked around and knew no one else in the kitchen saw him. He took my hand and pressed the outside edge onto the grill, smiling at me. The pain was there, but I was too focused on his intensity. And the piece of charred chin that just fell off his face didn't help my focus either. The smell of my own flesh was very appetizing.

"Oh shit, Chuck's hurt," Ramirez called out.

Washington and Conti ran over first. They desperately pulled my hand off the cooktop, but I resisted. Aurelio just stood there, burning a hole through me. Was he really holding my hand or was I doing it?

"You stupid asshole, get your fuckin' hand off the grill," Conti yelled as Washington tackled me to the ground.

Shit, they're going to flag me. I'd be out for weeks. I couldn't be away for that long. I looked at the blackened, bloodied mess that I once called my hand. I quickly put it to my mouth and tasted it. Like an unseasoned piece of pork. Little juicier than I expected.

"Get the first aid kit," Conti yelled out as Washington scrambled off the floor. "Come on, Chuck. You dumb fuck. Let's wash that off in the sink."

We went over to the sink, and the cool water flowed over my singed hand. I was disappointed to see that most of the char wasn't actually my skin but rather the grease from the grill. My hand was still burned pretty well—just enough to avoid a third-degree burn. Maybe I could coin the term *well-done second degree*?

Conti and Washington patched me up while Ramirez watched from his station. I saw fear in his eyes. That smart-ass, loud-mouthed little spic actually had feelings. *I'll be damned.* I always pinned him for some street-tough lackey to some bigger

Mexican. Like Chester and Spike from Looney Tunes. Didn't change my opinion of him much. He should be over here helping his fellow inmates clean me up. But he just stood there with his little brown dick in his hand.

"Ramirez, you're a little pussy fuck, you know that?"

His expression changed drastically. "You shut up. You *comadreja blanca*." White weasel. "Burning yourself like that."

I stumbled, but Conti and Washington helped me up, just as Schaeffer was making his way back into the room.

"What the hall happened here?" he asked.

"I burned my hand. No big deal. I'm fine."

"His hand is completely burned, Schaeffer." Washington ratted me out. "No way he's cooking with that for a while."

Schaeffer looked down at my hand. "Make a fist, Chuck."

I tried but winced at the pain.

"Yep, you're well done all right. Go home, Chuck."

"But . . ."

"Nope." He cut me off without hesitation. "You go home and rest up for a few days. Don't let me see you back here until you can make a fist."

Go home? Who the fuck is this string-bean jerkoff talking to?

"You never take your time off, so you'll be paid for it. No worries about that. But we'll hold down the kitchen until you're back."

"I can cook . . . really," I pleaded.

I hadn't been off from work since I started. There was an efficient process to get the food out. No one could lead this team like I did. The food would be overcooked, or worse, undercooked. Inmates might get sick, and they'd blame me for it.

The pacing of my thoughts got more intense. "Please, Schaeffer, you can't make me go home. I'll do anything." A tear started to slide down my cheek.

"You really love food that much, don't you?" he asked with great concern.

"It's all I got." I intensified my tone. "Now step aside and let me get back to work."

Schaeffer put a hand on my shoulder. "I'm going to ask you nicely once more, and then it's gonna get a little unpleasant. Keep in mind that there aren't any cameras back here. You walk out of here right now and take a few days off, and I won't report the injury or make it an issue with the warden. But if not, I'm going to smack the shit out of you and break that hand so you can't use it well ever again. I don't want to do it that way, but I will if I need to."

I'd been outmatched, and everyone knew it. For the first time since working with Conti, Washington, and Ramirez, they all watched in total silence. I'd embarrassed myself. Just like when I was little. Before I could mask my emotions and discomfort.

I rushed out of the kitchen and got to my car. I was having a lot of trouble regulating myself. My vision was blurred, stomach tight, and a cold sweat crept down the back of my neck. I wiped my eyes and grabbed the steering wheel.

What the hell am I going to do at home?

Chapter 11

That night, I lay on my little couch, in my little apartment, with the local news playing more stories about the Meadowsville incident. Nothing comforting about this place. No pictures, no decor, just functional items in a sterile environment. It used to be different. I had lots of possessions growing up. Tons of widgets and toys, and my room was filled to the brim. But my father was always very demanding of a tidy room. Like it was my stuff, but he always had the final say in how it all was used and stored.

"Put your shit away before I throw it out!"

"You live like a fucking pig."

"Do you wanna get sick?"

"I raised you better than this."

Even the way I ate was judged.

"You're eating too much!"

"Why aren't you eating enough?"

"Your mother isn't making anything else for dinner."

There would be times I would force myself to eat and end up vomiting it up later on. I made sure to clean it up, so no one ever knew. That was where my fascination with tasting myself really began. I never minded the flavor of my snot, my blood, puke, or anything else I materialized. Some of it was an acquired taste, but none of it was bad. I found myself purposely cutting myself to get another taste. Pulling skin off a scrape and eating it. Sometimes waiting until a scab hardened a bit before chewing on it for a while. If only my body could provide sustenance for itself. All those things Aurelio said to me in that cell. And then he encouraged me to take it a step further. I'd just been using myself as add ons. Never considered my body a complete meal until today.

But I hated food for so long. Wasn't until I learned to cook that I began to cherish it so much. All the textures and flavors that I spent my earlier years missing out on. No such thing as a gross food, just types that weren't prepared properly. Even that sludge in the prison, I could stylize to make it at least halfway edible. And I knew I could take anything and make it taste good. Myself included.

Renegade groomed himself on the floor, his eyes shut as he expressed zero concern about anything. All that mattered was that he was fed and groomed. I wonder if he would like how I tasted? Almost as quickly as the thought passed through my mind, the cat stopped, with his paw still lifted up, and stared me down.

"Don't worry, boy. I'm only enough man for myself."

I got up and swept the floor. I did it about twenty minutes ago, but I needed to move around a bit. I spent upward of twelve hours a day in that prison, pacing the kitchen. Cleaning, planning, preparing, cooking—there was always something to do. I couldn't just sit here with my thoughts. They were too painful. The memories needed to just stay in the past and stop making themselves known. It wasn't fair. I made it through to this point in my life in one piece. So why did I have to keep reliving all of that?

I swept up a single piece of cat litter and decided to sweep again. Just to be sure I didn't miss anything.

"Does that look clean to you, Chucky?" I heard my father barking at me.

I kept sweeping.

"Does it? I'm talking to you!" he yelled.

"It's fucking spotless!" I screamed, throwing the broom across the room.

Renegade jumped five feet in the air and looked at me in what I referred to as his action pose. Fur puffed out, a rounded back, wide eyes, and nails completely protracted.

I then noticed Aurelio, DeMarco, and Higgins were all in my kitchen. They stared at me in their undead forms, not uttering a single word. But I could tell when someone was hungry.

And they were watching me like a pack of hyenas.

Chapter 12

"What do you want from me?"

The three looked at one another before back to me, answering in total unison.

"We want to help you."

"With what?"

"We want to help you discover who you really are."

"Who am I?"

"You are the greatest gift that any kitchen could ever hope for."

I'm wasn't used to getting compliments. I only heard from people around me when I've made a mistake or didn't do something up to their standards. I looked at my hand, which was throbbing from the deep burn.

"Why are you being so mean to me?"

"It's for your own good, Chucky," I heard them say, as my father stated to me many, many times.

"I don't have much. Food is it. Without food, I am nothing. Food and I are one together. And if I can't cook, even for a single day, I have no purpose."

I was getting anxious and riled. My bones felt like they wanted to jump through my skin.

I walked to the kitchen and grabbed a chef's knife. I put it to my wrist. "Is this what you all want me to do? End it? Because I'm not some pussy who talks about it. I'll do it."

Renegade hissed from the other side of the apartment, clearly seeing the ghosts and feeling my angst.

"I don't deserve to be haunted by a couple of scumbag killers like you all were. I'll die before it gets to that." I pressed the knife to my wrist and began cutting downward.

The pain never bothered me.

Higgins began whispering in my ear, "You can't cut it, Chucky."

DeMarco on the other side. "No balls, this one."

Both of them repeated my father's abusive words to me, bringing me right back to feeling like a defenseless little boy again. I kept cutting, until the knife was lifted off my forearm. There was a growing wound, but the bleeding wasn't excessive as it spotted on the counter.

"You're so wasteful," I heard my father say.

I licked the counter and put the wound into my mouth, suckling on it like a baby to a mother's breast. The blood was just how it had always been. Reliable and satisfying.

Aurelio pulled my arm down and stuck his fleshy hand over my mouth. He grabbed the knife and pressed the blade against my right thigh. I had sharpened the blade a few weeks ago, so it could cut through most things with ease.

The sharpness lacerated my sweatpants, leaving a cold sensation on my skin. Then he began to move it back and forth, cutting at a slight angle. It entered my leg, and I ground my teeth to resist making a noise. He stared me right in the eyes, moving the knife with extreme precision. Warm blood poured down my leg. Then the knife came out, and his hand came off my face. It was then I noticed a chunk of my thigh sitting on the skillet, ready to be cooked.

Having a moment of clarity, I said, "I understand."

The three ghouls smiled.

Chapter 13

I woke up the following morning completely fatigued. The type of fatigue that made it hurt just to roll over in bed. I kicked my legs a bit to get the momentum to sit up. My arms felt like they were made of lead, my head like a drum being played, and my body like I ran a marathon. Almost took away from noticing the pain coming from my leg and my hand.

I recalled feeling a little fuzzy after the blood loss but being directed to cook my own flesh by the ghosts. I wanted to get the full extent of the flavor, so I just added some extra virgin olive oil, salt, and cracked pepper. It wasn't a big piece of meat, like a sliver of a filet mignon, but the flavor was like nothing I'd had to date. The appearance was like steak but had the consistency of veal. Went into the skillet red and came out gray. The seasoning was just right. The odor was also similar to pork, but with a little something else included. Just a unique experience.

I was sure that someone who saw my actions would've spoken to me with great conviction. Told me why I was truly mentally ill and needed to seek help. But if I was only hurting myself, then what was the harm? One day, I'd die, and they'd toss me in a hole so the bugs could eat me. Why should they have all the fun?

After all, I endured a childhood full of trauma. A hard, well-earned career that I accomplished all on my own. No training or formal education or any sort of nepotism to help me along. Just a love for food and a deep desire to make something of myself. I guess I took that goal a little too literally now.

Yesterday was a lot to handle. Between Crispy, Windchime, and Jab, my three persistent ghosts, I was feeling a little overwhelmed by everything that'd been happening since the Meadowsville incident. Whatever happened that day changed things. Maybe just for me, but I was sure there were others. Just had to be. But these ghosts . . . why were they making it a point to brutalize me? Like I was so privileged and had so much power and influence?

I wanted them to leave me alone. However, they were also pushing me to become something more than I could have imagined. Was my newfound curiosity for cannibalism something to be worried about? Again, I wasn't hurting anyone else, so I should be okay.

Even watching the executions—it wasn't for enjoyment. I didn't feel anything for the prisoners. They all made their choices and would take those decisions to the grave. Killing, raping, all of it was inexcusable, and that was why they were no longer suited to exist with the rest of us. I did look down on them. I might have my issues, but they were like rabid animals. Going out of their way to ruin the lives of others. That was ugly, disgusting stuff. Their families, neighbors, friends, and whoever else knew the victims all had their lives permanently altered. Selfish actions by a bunch of glorified animals. And for some reason, I had the spirits of a beaner, a marshmallow-looking pig, and a greased-up Guido all just following me around.

I stood up, and every part of my body buckled. Renegade was sunning himself in the middle of my living room, with the daylight brightening up his already pure white stomach. I wondered what cat would taste like. Probably like shit. Just like their attitudes.

I took my first step and I almost fell. I caught myself on the bed. My leg was very sore from the wound. I looked down and saw it was covered in dried blood that made a nice, large trail down to my foot. The cut was very clean but clearly infected. I looked at the rest of the house, and it was spotless. I guessed ghosts cleaned too? But those miserable cocksuckers couldn't clean up my leg?

I limped to the bathroom, nearly falling over the toilet, and managed to find the edge of the bathtub.

"Ah, the price of perfection," I said to myself.

I put the water on, letting it wash out the cut. It stung, but I could handle the pain. The number of times I've massacred my body cooking in that prison over the years was insane. So much scar tissue all over and a very high tolerance for pain.

Using my hand, I lathered up some soap and pressed it into the wound, trying to clean out all the dried blood. I had it clean in just under a minute, but it started bleeding again. And there was no towel nearby.

"Fuck," I said out loud.

I kicked the small bathroom rug to the wall in order not to track blood all over it. I stood up, putting pressure on the gash to reduce the flow, but it poured out. The white floor became a crimson mess. And then I just observed the red fluid. That much blood could really serve me well in a stew. I became momentarily distracted by food and slipped on the blood, collapsing to the floor.

The wind was knocked out of me, and I lay there, staring at the chipped paint on the ceiling. I took some shallow breaths and closed my eyes, still feeling the blood coming out. I moved my arms and legs, and they slid around. I opened my eyes and saw Higgins, DeMarco, and Bazalar leering down at me. My entire body was smeared with my own blood. They watched me like I was a Thanksgiving dinner. I wiped my hand across the floor and rubbed it over my mouth.

"Tastes so good," I said to myself as I blacked out.

"It sure does, Chucky," all three apparitions said in unison.

Chapter 14

I woke up to being ten years old again. My father sat across from me. His barrel chest heaved, and he was crunching on what looked to be fingers. My fingers. I looked at my hand, but everything was intact, including my gnawed-down fingernails.

He watched me with that look. I couldn't tell if he was content or upset. Angry or tired. Always a scary mystery to guess what mood and mindset the old man was in. He picked up a pinky finger and crunched down, with some blood dripping down the one side of his mouth.

"Eat up, Chucky. Your mom ain't making you anything else. Thought you liked ladyfingers for dinner."

I loathed that nickname. Made me cringe each and every time. I looked at my mom, who was eating in slow motion. It was just him and me.

"They're not ladyfingers. They're my fingers," my prepubescent voice sputtered out. My mouth trembled a bit.

"That's what I said. *Ladyfingers*. Because you're a little lady. Aren't ya, Chucky?"

"No, I'm going to grow up big and strong. And I'm going to eat what I want one day."

My father chuckled, looking down at his plate.

How could there be so many fingers?

"I thought you loved when your mom made special meals for you. After all, you wanted ladyfingers for dinner tonight." He spit a fingernail out onto the floor. "Now all you can do is sit here and bitch about it. You little prima donna."

I went to talk back, knowing this was a dream, but it felt so real, and I just couldn't. I noticed my mother had completely frozen in place now. Like a painted statue.

He pounded the table and shook the room like an earthquake. I quickly put one into my mouth. It was moist and had a soggy texture. I bit down, and my teeth penetrated each level of tissue from the skin to the muscle and finally bone. The bone was too hard and almost cracked my teeth. But the rest of it was delicious. He still watched me. Every movement I made, he was watching me. Judging me. Waiting for the perfect opportunity to degrade me. To make me feel like a piece of garbage.

A nothing. And, worst of all, I actually believed it. And that angered me most of all. I spit out the bone.

"Eat your goddamned dinner, Chucky," his monstrous voice bellowed out, shaking me to the core of my soul.

He suddenly looked bigger and meaner. His eyes turned bloodshot and his pupils into a shade darker than midnight. His shoulders heaved, and I was so much smaller. Like a mouse to a cat now.

The warmth of my own urine ran down my leg. The warmth was soothing, in a way. Then, I realized it wasn't urine. It was blood. I looked up, and he was looming over me with a face so frightful that I started to cry. Then I jumped awake. Still on the bathroom floor, covered in blood. I was still crying.

My leg finally clotted, but some minor remnants of blood were still coming out. I finally found a towel and applied pressure. I looked into the living room, and Renegade was staring at me. Just an uncaring, unconcerned stare. Like he was laughing inside or totally uninterested in my struggle. Just like Dad.

"Fucking cat," I muttered, trying to stop the bleeding with one hand and wipe my tears away with the other. I wondered again how a cat tasted. Braised might be good. Or maybe roasted. Few viable options. I mean, 1.4 billion chinks couldn't be wrong, right? *You can't be judged by something you can eat.* Including yourself. Hmm . . . that was an odd thought.

I managed to stand up, keeping the towel against my leg. I could no longer tell what was tears versus sweat. My body felt warm from the adrenaline rush. I barely acknowledged the burned areas of my hand. They were inconsequential.

I gently washed myself down and cleaned the bathroom. I remember cleaning up cum, piss, shit, vomit, and drugs when I first started working in restaurants. The bathrooms were worse than anyone could imagine. People were disgusting, fucking pigs. No care in the world for anyone but themselves. Do what they wanted, whenever they wanted. And people like me were left to clean up after them, just trying to learn a trade and make an honest living. It was no wonder I had a lack of empathy for my fellow man. Watching them hang, sizzle, twitch, and all the other ways Eagle Stone was allowed to execute the inmates just gave me a certain satisfaction. Like there was one less piece of garbage on the streets. One less person that could potentially harm me. Make fun of me. Make me feel like I did when I lived at home as a child.

They were all the same. They were just different types of meat all hanging from hooks for me to view. Each of them waiting to be prepared for death in a different way. And I got to show them how talented I was before they left this earth. I got to show them they didn't have any effect on me. No matter what their misdeeds or taunts were, I was still able to thrive. I wanted them all to taste the perfection I crafted for them. One final way for me to show them I was better. And I would outlast them. Like a cockroach or a Twinkie, I would always survive. Even the most deplorable conditions. No one would ever control me again.

Chapter 15

Several days later, I returned to work. My thigh was heavily bandaged, leaving me with a slight limp, but my hand was mostly pain free. All those years burning myself and scrubbing dishes with scalding hot water really did toughen them up.

Conti, Washington, and Ramirez all prepped the grills for the breakfast rush. Eggs being cracked and hitting the grill, low-grade toast being burned in the ovens, orange juice that was glorified piss water, coffee brewing, and little packets of jelly and butter being tossed in a beautiful rhythm onto the serving trays. The radio played in the background, with the morning news continuing to cover the Meadowsville incident. All the surrounding towns and cities were taking bodies in to try to identify them all. Whatta mess.

"I'm not that bad off. I can man the grills, Conti," I said.

"Nope, Schaeffer gave us orders to not let you touch anything until that hand is one hundred percent."

"It is," I quickly responded, making a fist but ultimately gritting my teeth.

"And that's why I gave the orders," Schaeffer cut in, slapping me on the shoulder. "You forget that I'm assigned to you. Can't let anything happen to my Chuck." He looked at my hand. "Geez, look at those char marks. I've seen less on a well-done burger. Be glad you don't have a lady. She'd hate those rough hands."

I wasn't in the mood for our usual banter, so I let it go. He meant well. Even Ramirez, who was a yappy little jumping bean, wasn't a bad guy. He worked his ass off and wanted to get back to his mamacitas and half dozen kids, I was sure.

"How's your wife tolerate you?" I asked.

"Look at these hands." He put them in front of me.

They were pale and veiny, which no discernable markings.

"These beauties are what makes her go wild. Baby smooth and highly skilled." He used two fingers to mimic finger banging.

I rolled my eyes at the crude gesture.

"Oh, and you'll be happy to know that we have another special meal request." Schaeffer handed me the standard yellow form.

Suddenly, my mood shifted. I looked at the request and saw that the inmate, Bert Bishop, wanted fried chicken, mashed potatoes, corn, and a brownie. How original. Might as well defrost him a fucking TV dinner. At least he had a cool-sounding name. It was a shit ton better than Chuck Saunders.

"This a black guy?"

"What does it matter?"

I guess it didn't. But that was a black-sounding name.

"When is this due by?"

"Tomorrow. He's set for execution in two days."

I nodded and put the form in my pocket. I'd honor it, despite not being much of a challenge. "I'm on it, boss," I grumbled sarcastically.

Schaeffer manned his usual post at the kitchen door as we all got to work.

"Schaeffer," I called out. "What's the method they chose for him?"

"The dogs," he said. "And for what he was convicted of, he deserves nothing less."

As we went through the meal services over the next ten hours, I managed to forget about the pain from my leg and even my hand. I had another assignment, and that was the most important thing. I had to request buttermilk, but already had everything else for the meal. Not sure who was going to enjoy the taste of the meal more, Bert Bishop or the dogs that were going to rip his innards out. Wait, didn't chocolate give dogs diarrhea? Not my problem. The janitors who worked the kennels on the other side of the prison could have their fun with that. I didn't mean for that to sound racist, but I guess it came across that way. No one can crack any jokes about skin color anymore. Not even a blanquito (white boy) like me.

Damn that Ramirez. I'm picking up that stupid Spanglish of his.

The next day was like a blur. Being at the prison almost twelve hours per day tended to have that effect. Besides running an errand or two, going home to sleep, and watching Renegade gracefully mock me in my own home, that was about all I had time for. And that was fine. Food was my life and should, therefore, take up majority of my time.

I had left the chicken to marinate in some salted buttermilk for several hours. Good to tenderize it. One of the pustules from my burned hand opened up and got some fluid on the chicken pieces as I dredged each portion, but that didn't matter. Bishop should be thankful to enjoy a small taste of what I have to offer. As painful as all of my outings had been, using parts of myself for different dishes, the flavor and satisfaction were worth the efforts.

The saying "Sometimes you have to burn the village to win the war" came to mind. And it was fairly accurate. Through pain came pleasure. I think Pinhead said that in one of the *Hellraiser* films. Smart cookie. A little pale for my taste, but I dug its vibes.

The oil in the fryer was ready to go, and I carefully dropped each chicken piece in. Ten to twelve minutes for the thighs and eight to ten for the drumsticks. Golden brown and then drain. As the chicken fried, I had a small pot of cubed potatoes in some boiling water. Little milk, salt, pepper, and butter tossed in before I mashed it all up. Easy stuff. The corn was also steaming in some salted water on the stovetop. The small tray of brownies was left cooling on the counter.

The kitchen was empty, except for me. The spirits of Aurelio, Higgins, and DeMarco weren't in the room with me, for once. Hadn't seen them in a few days, but that at least let me recover from my injuries.

Schaeffer poked his head into the kitchen to see if everything was ready, like an impatient husband waiting for his wife to get a meal on the table. *Perfection takes time, Mr. Schaeffer, you bull-nosed fuck.* About twenty minutes later, everything was cooked and plated. My assigned officer and I traveled through the prison, hearing the same taunts from all these jungle rats. Them getting to smell the food I prepared was more than any of them deserved. I hoped every last one of these people got hanged, mauled, or shot. And I wanted to see every one of them die. *Choke on those mean words as you leave this earth.* I would be the last thing on their mind before it went dark.

We entered the cell of Bishop, who was a large, burly man with a handlebar mustache. He was shackled to the floor, sitting at a small table, bolted to the ground.

"Prisoner Bishop, I present to you your last meal." As I finished saying it, Bazalar, Higgins, and DeMarco stood in the back of the room, just observing.

Oh, Jesus fuck, are they about to enlist Bishop to haunt me too?

"Thank you, sir," Bishop stated as he looked at my meal with the most crystal-clear eyes. "This looks amazing."

Huh, look at that. Someone finally showed me some gratitude. *I'll be dipped in shit.* Almost brought a tear to my eye. I thought I was the only one who appreciated my food all this time. I looked up and saw DeMarco mouth the same words to me. I knew he was being sarcastic when he said it all those weeks ago. Just like how Dad used to put down Mom's cooking. Never thanked her. For anything. He would only talk to her when he wanted something or she did something not up to some standard he had. No excuse for that shit.

Bishop dove right into his meal. I figured for a guy his size, he'd be a sloppy eater, but he was actually quite delicate. A little fast but still gentle. I wondered how my pus added to the chicken flavor. I should've taken a bite before plating it. But, then again, that would be disrespectful to the inmate and the dish. I'd have other chances.

"Gosh, this is amazing. Best meal I've ever had."

A smile stretched across my face, and Schaeffer took notice of it.

"Good for you, Chuck," he whispered.

Something I never had the ambition to do prior hit me like a jolt of lightning. "Good luck tomorrow, Bishop."

He looked up to me with a tear in his eye and smiled. The most pleasant prisoner meal I've dealt with in all the years here. I didn't know what to do with the satisfaction this gave me. I felt good and elated, but what to do with that from here? Oh well, back to the kitchen I went. I looked back one more time and saw the three apparitions still there also smiling at me.

What the hell do they want from me?

Chapter 16

I sat in the viewing area, as Bishop was in a small space. He didn't look like he was afraid of his imminent death. The dogs growled and barked from beyond the door. Warden Monroe's voice came over the loudspeaker. "Robert Bishop. Found guilty of multiple counts of rape against a minor and first-degree murder. He is sentenced to death by canine. May God have mercy on your soul."

Such tactful verbiage from the warden, but that lisp always made me laugh. Guy was as cold as an ice cube. I didn't believe in vampires, but if they did exist, he would be one. Made me think of Kurt Barlow from Stephen King's *Salem's Lot*. He was rarely seen but was always present for executions. I honestly only spoke to him during my interview, and it was extremely awkward. Not like I was applying for a job, but almost like I was pleading for my life. Maybe that was his way of weeding out anyone who couldn't handle the pressure of the job. The long hours, limited time off, the population at hand. Not for the weak at heart.

Bishop didn't run or try to escape. Not like it would've done any good, anyway. He stood there, looking up toward the viewing room. Toward me. I felt that gaze directly on me. He smiled, not in a malicious way but in a sincere, coming-to-terms-with-this-situation sort of smile. Like he was at peace. Maybe I was to thank for that?

The door to the kennel opened, and five huge pit bulls ran out. They dove on him, instantly knocking him to the ground. They looked ravenous as they took chunks out of his flesh. One grabbed his neck and tugged at the skin for a few seconds, fighting off two of the others for the prized spot. Bishop's clothes were torn to shreds, and the dogs feasted on his innards, which were pulled out like chew toys. A solid lump of skin was bitten off his leg, exposing the muscle and bone. The dog on his neck finally bit through, and blood squirted several feet from the body. A pool developed underneath the body as the dogs licked it up and continued gnawing at Bishop. He was deceased at that point, and the strangest thing was he never screamed or fought back. It was possibly the most peaceful execution I ever saw.

The door to the kennel reopened, and the dogs dropped the body and ran back to their designated holding areas. They were covered in blood and just had a hardy meal. Bishop's body was a pile of gore, left there like nothing.

LAST MEAL

With no reactions from the few people in the viewing room, each person stood up and left. And, to no surprise, as soon as I stood up, I saw Bishop standing by the doorway. He looked exactly as he did when I served him his last meal. Well, almost the same. Just with a few bite marks and blood splotches.

"Oh great, another one to deal with," I said to myself.

Why couldn't that bullshit in Meadowsville happen after I wasn't around anymore, whatever the fuck it triggered around here. Like I didn't have enough problems.

Now I'm being harassed and assaulted by death-row inmate ghosts. Unbelievable. This crap's for the birds.

Chapter 17

That night, I got home and stood in the bathroom. I stared at my body. A pudgy belly, thick, pigtail-like hair sprouting out all over, no muscular definition anywhere, scars all over from self-mutilation in the name of high-end cuisine, and a face that only a mother could love. Maybe I should ask for reduced hours at the prison. I could take some time and take care of myself. Little exercise and some self-care wouldn't hurt, would it? Then again, if I weren't there for every meal, each day of the week, who the hell knew what kind of scum would tarnish that kitchen. They'd probably get some fry cook to cover whatever gap I left. I was sure Conti, Washington, and Ramirez would love getting me out of there though.

I leaned into the mirror and pulled the skin down around the base of my eyes. Dark, wrinkled pockets. "You look like shit, Chucky boy," I said to myself.

"Yeah, some push-ups will make everything better," DeMarco said from behind me.

"Or better yet, how about some crunches to get that tummy flat?" Higgins chimed in.

"I like my meat with a nice layer of fat on it. No changes needed by me," Bazalar said as they all started to laugh.

"I appreciate the concern, you ghouls. How come I don't hear your new friend?" I turned to see Bishop standing away from what I should probably dub *the three spooketeers*.

"Nothing from you, Bishop?" I asked, seeing him staring off toward the ceiling.

"Nothing from me, boss," he replied calmly.

I turned on the shower, uncaring if the ghosts enjoyed my nudity or not. After all, it was my home. They were trespassing. Spiritual trespassers. Not too far off from illegal aliens, which we definitely didn't need more of in this country. Just like my dad used to tell me, "If it ain't white, it ain't right." Never positive that I completely agreed with that, but it was the least of my worries. You don't always have to change all the programming in your head from childhood.

"Take all those taxes out of my fucking paychecks to support those wetbacks," I murmured, lost in my thoughts.

I flinched as the water ran down my body. I felt the burn on the hand, the gash in the thigh, and all the other damage that I'd been doling out to myself lately. I must be fucking gone. Cooking parts of myself. What the fuck was I thinking?

"Don't take too long in there, Chuck," Higgins taunted.

"Eat shit, dead head," I replied.

I carefully lathered a washcloth and wiped my body down. There was always an odor of food that was stuck to me, no matter how hard I'd scrub or whatever products I used to cover it. Probably why I was an incel. What woman would want to talk to an out-of-shape, miserable, racist loner who chronically stank of prison food? Although there were some weird fetishes out there. What was that song, "Freaks Come Out at Night"? Well, maybe they did, but not here. Nor would they ever. I was just left beating my meat like it owed me money. Or, better yet, shucking my corn. Gosh, corn was so tasty. *Now I'm hungry.*

"You ain't jerking off in there, are ya?" Bazalar called out. "If ya are, get that thing nice and bloody. We can peel it like a carrot and find something new to cook with it."

These sick fucking puppies. I couldn't be haunted by friendly ghosts like Casper. No, I had these three, who took pride in not just haunting me but promoting my own self-harm.

"Thank you, Aurelio. I'm so glad you didn't fall off the banana boat when your parents came here years ago. I'm so blessed to have you in my life," I sarcastically called out.

He returned fire. "You racist pile of dog shit. I should cut you into little pieces and feed you to a stray dog. Plenty to go around."

I shut off the shower and pushed my hand deep into the cut on my leg. I forced it into the wound until the blood started coating my fingers, dribbling down my leg with the water. I whipped open the curtain and faced all four specters. I wiped the blood across my chest in a symbolic and defensive way. "You're lucky I'm not dead or you're not still alive. Or else we'd go. You and me. Win, lose, or draw, I'd teach you some fuckin manners."

Aurelio pushed me backward, and I slipped, landing headfirst in the bathtub. The pain made me feel nauseous, and I couldn't see straight. My legs stuck out, and my upper body was trapped.

I heard all three ghosts say in unison, "You never had much manners, Chucky." But still nothing from Bishop.

That's my dad. I don't know what this all is, but somehow he's involved. I hate that fucking nickname.

I tried desperately to sit up, but my arms weren't strong enough. I grunted, and my vision somewhat returned, albeit very blurry. I saw a trail of red running down the tub. More blood from me. I'd add this to the ever-growing list of injuries. I tried again to push myself up, but the lingering pain from my burned hand caused me to wince. I slipped and smacked the head injury one more time on the tub. I closed my eyes and began to wiggle my body into the tub. I was still wet enough to maneuver myself in. Against all odds, I made it happen. I sat in the bathtub and opened my eyes. Between my leg wound, head injury, and the pain in my hand, I couldn't move much more. I allowed myself to slip into a slumber. Maybe I would wake up. Maybe I wouldn't.

Not sure which to hope for anymore.

Chapter 18

I woke up hours later. The bleeding seemed to have stopped, and I saw only Bishop in the corner, still not looking at me. I wondered where the other three toads went.

"Bishop, can you help me?" I asked, hoping he obliged.

He walked over and gave me a hand, getting me to my feet. Christ almighty, did my head hurt.

"The more you let them bully you, the worse this gets."

I wasn't sure what to make of that.

I limped to the sink and looked at my blurred image. "Maybe you're right. But there's not much I can do when I can't control or even touch them." I took out a hand mirror and reflected it off the mounted wall mirror to get a glimpse of the damage done to my head. I saw a very moist pocket of blood with a chunk of skin hanging off.

"If you want to stop them, just take control," Bishop said, handing me a pair of kitchen shears. "Remember, they can't hurt you if you don't let them."

I understood what he meant. And I was tired of the hauntings. It was exhausting. No one could make me feel any specific way. That was for me to decide—embarrassment, anger, hate, any of it.

I took the scissors from him and positioned the flap of my scalp against the blade. To smother the noise, I bit down on a small hand towel.

"The power is in your hands. And no one else's," Bishop said in my ear.

I could almost feel the bristle of his ridiculous mustache.

He was right. He was absolutely 100 percent right. I'd never felt like I had the power to do much, except for cooking. Dad always made that clear to me. I needed to toughen up and take charge. Or I'd get pissed on in life. Oh, and cooking was for faggots, apparently. He was such a kind soul. So loving and considerate of other people's feelings. It was no wonder I didn't even go to his funeral.

But maybe I could solve it all with one ambition. I'd been tiptoeing along in this journey of mine for too long. I loved to cook, and I loved the way I tasted. Why should I deny myself the greatest gift I could provide for me? All for me, just for me.

I snapped the scissors, and the pain brought me out of the probable concussive state. I screamed into the washcloth as Renegade looked in from the living room, wide-eyed and terrified. I felt sweat and blood running down the fat flaps on my back, trickling down further and further until it began to tickle the backs of my thighs.

I looked down at the hairy chunk of flesh. My mind already tickled itself with the possibilities of how it could be prepared.

I put compression on the gushing wound on my head, ignoring the pain. I looked around, and I was left alone again. I hated ghosts. I fucking hated all ghosts. And they were not going to control me anymore.

Chapter 19

I stood over a cutting board. The discoloration was beyond reproach, but the jail wouldn't allow me to replace it until the start of the new year. So it'd just have to do. Washington, Conti, and Ramirez all minded their manners while Schaffer played with his key ring. Just a quiet, organized day in the kitchen.

I looked at a large, girthy parsnip and began peeling it. I recalled doing the same thing the night before in my kitchen. Taking all my hair off. Touching my own skin but not feeling anything, as it was no longer part of my body. Such an empowering experience. Like I was more than just a person. I was a food source and beacon of creativity. And then I boiled the scalp meat. It didn't look appetizing at first, but after I added truffle oil to it, atop a pile of fettuccine noodles, it was worthy of at least a two-star Michelin rating.

As I was about to cut the parsnip, someone grabbed my hand. I looked up, and it was Bazalar again. He was forcing the knife over my pinky finger, not taking his eyes off mine. I resisted as much as I could, but he was too strong. He pushed the knife down, and it severed the very top of the finger. I didn't break eye contact. I wasn't afraid anymore. I didn't flinch and I didn't react. I simply took the knife and cut down the finger a little further. One chop and half of my pinky was gone.

"You have nothing over me anymore, Dad," I said to him, making Bazalar smile and nod. I understood what this was now.

"Oh fuck, Schaeffer, he's doing it again," Conti called out.

Schaeffer grabbed the knife out of my hand and raised my arm over my head. I didn't resist. I just let it happen. I'd proven my point to all of them. And who would have thought that one of these garbage prisoners would have been the one to give me full clarity of mind.

"Call the infirmary. *Now!*" Schaeffer barked.

I started to feel warm and tired. I lost consciousness, suddenly seeing the four ghosts watching over me, smiling. Bishop now seemed right at home with the others.

Chapter 20

I woke up hours later. I was so disoriented, with all the accidents lately, that I wasn't even sure what day it was. Schaeffer and Warden Monroe sat near my bed in the infirmary.

I tried to sit up, but my body was in shambles. Everything hurt. And I must have hit my head again when I passed out. My leg, hand, head, finger, everything had been properly treated.

"Mr. Saunders," Warden Monroe started. "You've had quite a lot of incidents lately."

God, that lisp.

"Yeah, yeah, I guess I have, Warden," I replied, knowing this was not going to end well.

"You've been with us for a long time. Far longer than any previous people we brought in during my tenure."

"Just about fifteen years," Schaeffer added in.

"Never one issue or injury. Then suddenly, all of this happened." He stood up and walked toward one of the windows. "Maybe we've worked you too hard. Or maybe it's just a buildup of the stress over the years. I'm not sure."

"I think—" I started, but he quickly cut me off.

"You've become a liability here, Mr. Saunders. And from what the nurses shared with me, you have multiple other self-inflicted injuries that they found too."

I stayed quiet. *I'm fired. I know it. Shit!*

"I will be sure to fund your pension for your years of service. You don't have the age yet to take any of it, but it'll be there when you reach that point."

I couldn't breathe. I needed this job. It was all I had. Then I remembered my new goal. I would be in total control of myself. I was bigger than this job.

I pulled the IV out of my wrist and licked it clean. My blood tasted as sweet as a bold red wine.

The warden and Schaeffer looked at me in shock.

"You know what, Warden, I think you're right. I've outgrown this place. I'm destined for something else."

I pulled all of the various electrodes and wires off my body and stood up. I was in agonizing pain, but I would walk out of here under my own power. I collected my things, got dressed, and walked out of the prison. It was a bittersweet thing. I'd miss this place. The hours sucked and the schedule was grueling, but it was what I worked so hard to get to. However, I needed to evolve. I could no longer live to serve others and be their final peace before death. I needed to serve the one person who mattered most. Me.

I wanted to see so many more people die. It gave me a sense of satisfaction and self-worth that wasn't easily explained. They died, and I was the very last thing that brought them pleasure. And I'd done it for hundreds of death-row inmates. Some decapitated, others fried like catfish nuggets, and each one was a nice ending to a tragic life. That was something to admire, wasn't it? They died due to their own actions. The ones who claimed innocence were liars. They all did something bad and faced the consequences.

I had nothing left. I'd reached my peak. Like a pot roast hitting an internal temperature of 145 degrees, I was cooked. Nothing left but to serve out my sentence.

Get it? Serve?

Chapter 21

I lay in my apartment. No noise, no routine, no anything. Just myself with my feelings. Probably the worst situation imaginable. I sat up and watched Renegade cleaning himself. I was no better than him. I now just existed with no purpose.

There was a knock at my door. Perhaps it was finally the grim reaper come to take me away. Death couldn't be that bad. Not worse than life. I refused to believe it.

I limped over and opened it to see Officer Schaeffer step in.

"Come in." I waved my hand sarcastically.

He looked around my apartment. "Well, Chuck, it's definitely you."

"What's that mean?"

"Bland and unappealing."

"Touché, Schaeffer." We both sat across from one another.

"I spoke to Warden Monroe. Said if you completed an in-patient program, he'll reconsider your job situation. But there's no negotiating that stipulation."

I sat back and laughed obnoxiously.

"Best I can do, Chuck. No one wants you to go. But you're dangerous now. Can't do this kinda stuff in there. Been too many times."

Did he miss me? Was that what this was?

"Look," he continued, "I'm not telling you what to do, but working with you for so long, I know how much you love it there. And Ramirez has been running his mouth something awful without you there to check him too."

I laughed. Maybe I should go back. But, then again, maybe they didn't deserve me back. If I went back there, what kind of message would that send? It'd let the warden know he could piss all over my face and I'd just smile and take it. As soon as I said yes to the treatment, that'd just be the start of the regulations he'd hammer me with. It was a trap. A nasty little trap he wanted to get me caught in. I deserved better. No one would have me under their thumb ever again.

"I appreciate the offer, Schaeff, but I can't do it."

He looked disappointed. "So that's it?"

"That's it."

"What are you gonna do with yourself?"

I sat in silence briefly. "Let's just say that I'm going to finally make something of myself."

We looked at one another for another minute.

"Well, old friend, I wish you luck." He leaned forward and shook my hand. "You're one odd person, Chuck Saunders. But you were a rockstar in that kitchen. And they'll all realize it when it sinks in that you're really gone."

He was right. They'd miss me only when I was gone. Everyone would.

Schaeffer stood up and made his way to the door, but something niggled at my mind. I never knew his first name.

"Schaeff, hang on."

He halted.

"What's your first name?"

"Bob." He smiled in a showing of respect.

"It was good working with you, Bob," I replied.

"Take care of yourself, Chuck. I'll be back to check on you in a few days."

And then he was gone. The last link to that place. Except the ghosts, who had been absent since I took on my new attitude. Maybe this was a blessing in disguise.

Chapter 22

I woke up late that night. The house was dead quiet, then I heard something in the kitchen. I got up and limped outside. I saw Bishop cleaning the kitchen. Nothing preternatural or strange, aside from the obvious. Just rags and cleaning products. He stopped and looked at me.

"Good morning, sweetie," he said, which made me tremendously uncomfortable.

"What? What are you saying? What is this?" I asked him.

"Tell me you haven't figured all this out yet. You were always so smart but could never see what was right in front of you sometimes. Even as a little boy."

It then occurred to me that Bishop had been kind to me through his particular haunting. The others were overpowering and nasty and violent, but he never joined in. This wasn't Bishop. This was Mom. She was looking out for me. A ghost possessing another ghost. Who the hell knew that was even possible? The Meadowsville incident really did blur the lines between our world and beyond. Maybe it made things strangely better. Brought up those unresolved feelings I tried to ward off all this time. Forced me to finally deal with it all. I knew this would happen one day. I couldn't keep running from it. I just never knew when or how.

A tear streaked down my face. I hadn't thought about her much since she died ten years ago. It was too painful. She lived as a victim and died as one too. Heart disease took her out at a young age. And part of me always wondered if she wanted to die because she felt like she let me down and couldn't live with herself. She just had no fight left in her. And she died quickly after my dad. Like she had to stick it out and never leave me alone with him, even as an adult. She was always proud of me. No matter how lowly my jobs were, she was always the diamond absolute in my life. When she left, she took a part of me with her. But here she was, right in front of my eyes.

"Hi, Charlie." Bishop's form now resembled Mom just as I remembered her. "Look what you've done to yourself, my baby boy."

It wasn't coming from a place of condemnation. It was concern, above all else.

I wanted to run over and hug her, but I knew that it wasn't possible. My lip trembled ever so slightly.

"Momma, I missed you so much." I started openly crying.

I hated this feeling. I vowed that I'd never cry again after she died, but here we were.

She gently caressed my cheek in a way that only a mother could. I looked at her, savoring the moment.

"I wish I could have done more for you," she said. "He was so mean to you. He made you so angry and hateful. But I always knew you were so much more."

"You did all you could, Mom. That took me a long time to understand, but I do now. It would have been worse to leave." I took a deep breath. "I'm not mad at you anymore. You did the right thing." When those words escaped my mouth, it felt like a giant rock was taken off my chest.

Peace didn't feel so bad after all.

She smiled kindly at me and gave me a hug. "I know I'm too late."

"For what?"

"For what's about to happen."

Somehow, she already knew what I was planning to do.

"I cleaned the kitchen so it was all ready for you, my sweet, sweet boy."

So even the spirit world knew what my destiny was. Just fucking great. There was no backing down now. The stars were aligned, and it was time to finish my plan.

"Thank you, Momma. I love you so much." I continued to sob.

"I love you, too, Charlie." She hugged me once more and disappeared.

The hug was so cold. Not the same warmth she had when she was alive. I was sadder than ever but grateful for the blessing from her. And I was alone again. Until I saw Bazalar, DeMarco, and Higgins all standing over me. They smashed their heads together, and a brilliant flash happened. Swear to God, it almost blinded me.

I looked up to see the ghostly apparition of my father. My sadness grew to confidence. I was no longer scared. And he had nothing over me, nor would he ever again.

Those big, crooked teeth smiled at me, and I could tell he wanted a front-row seat.

"Cooking was always for faggots, son. And you'll die a faggot too."

I sighed in relief, as the words no longer impacted me. "That's where you're wrong. You just never could see past your own problems. You could never see how talented and dedicated I was. You always just felt inferior to me and took it out on me and Mom. You will no longer haunt me, in this world or beyond. Because I'm going to finish this once and for all. I hope you linger in purgatory forever, you abusive prick."

As soon as I was done speaking, all ghosts were gone. I didn't feel anything except motivation to cook. My brain and body were so beyond repair that I had no choice. I was going to make my own last meal. And it would be from myself. The most satisfying final treat I could imagine. A miserable, shitty life ended in total glory. Something never done before. I would be a legend. How about that? Chuck Saunders would be a legend.

And no one would think this was a happy ending, but to me, it would be the happiest finale possible.

The pressure grew, as I only had one shot at this. I wanted to taste every part of myself, like a sampler. And I needed it to be comforting. I wanted a nice Chuck stew.

I rummaged through the cabinets and found beef stock, followed by paprika, pepper, and Worcestershire sauce. I lined them up on the counter and then pulled out some slightly aged carrots, onions, celery, and potatoes. This was going to be a feast. All for me.

I took out my trusty stockpot and filled it with the ingredients, chopping and mincing like a master chef. Now came the trickiest part.

I took my sharpest cutting knife and held it up to my right cheek. I pressed in until I felt the knife penetrate to my tongue. I turned it and sliced a hole out of my cheek. Cheek meat was the most tender part of a pig, and I couldn't see why I would be any different. I licked the perimeter of the wound, feeling a cool breeze every time I breathed in and out. The pain was barely there. I was beyond physical discomfort now. I had a lifetime of preparing for this.

I tossed the cheek meat into the pot, just as the first bubbles were starting to rise up, signaling a low boil. I then cut a deep cube out of my shoulder, then a deep cut from my abdomen, my upper arm, and my thigh, then my calf. Nice, healthy chunks of Chuck. I was starting to feel a bit dizzy as blood was pooling at my feet, but I wasn't going to let it stop me. My body screamed in pain, but my mind and spirit were in total harmony. I performed each cut no differently than a butcher dissecting a cow to harvest the meat.

All the meat went into the pot as I mixed it. The stew began to boil, and the room smelled like such a unique odor. Then I stuck my tongue out and used the kitchen shears to lob off a piece of the rear left side, plopping it into the mix. That was the area of the tongue that detected sour tastes, so it wouldn't affect my savoring of this dish. I allowed everything to simmer for about twenty minutes at a higher-than-desired temperature. I was working against the clock, in case anyone didn't know.

I gargled with the blood in my mouth and spit it into the stew. The beef stock wasn't enough—I needed to add some more liquid, and fast. This was the big moment of no return. I put the knife along my anterior forearm and sliced right along the artery, following the scar from the recent cut. The blood pooled out rather quickly as I directed it over the pot. It added a deep hue to the broth and made the room smell of a mild sweetness. I had about five minutes before I passed out from all the blood loss.

Renegade came over, obviously liking the smell of this meal too.

"Renegade, you're . . . in for . . . a treat." I jumbled some of the words from the blood in my mouth.

A few short minutes later, I was barely holding on, but the stew looked done. The meat chunks were cooked, as were the vegetables.

LAST MEAL

I spooned it into two bowls and slumped against the cabinets, guiding myself to the ground. I put the one bowl in front of Renegade, who ate quicker than any animal in the history of the world. He actually looked like he was smiling. I pet his little head and watched him clean himself and go back to his sleeping spot on the couch.

"I hope you find a better home than this one, bud."

Now was the moment of truth. I took my spoon and slurped the Chuck stew. It was the most delicious, unique dish I'd ever had. I was able to chew a few pieces of meat but couldn't tell which was what part. It didn't matter. It was so good. I mean, *I* was so good. Then I took one last look at Renegade as my eyes closed.

I smiled as I felt myself slip into death. "I won," I whispered.

About the Author

I am an author, reviewer, and horror fanatic. I am also an accomplished, self-taught chef and baker, a proud father and husband, and a clinical exercise physiologist by trade.

Connect with me
https://www.facebook.com/topsidepeter
https://www.instagram.com/ptopside/
https://twitter.com/PTopside
https://www.bookbub.com/authors/peter-topside
https://www.goodreads.com/author/show/19743489.Peter_Topside

Also by Peter Topside

The Preternatural Trilogy:
Preternatural (Book 1)
Preternatural Reckoning (Book 2)
Preternatural Evolution (Book 3)

Love and Pieces

www.ingramcontent.com/pod-product-compliance
Lightning Source LLC
LaVergne TN
LVHW041532070526
838199LV00046B/1623